Rain, Rain, Go Away

by James Preller

Illustrated by
Duendes Del Sur

SCHOLASTIC INC.
New York Toronto London Auckland Sydney
Mexico City New Delhi Hong Kong

Hopsalot the Rabbit was happy.
He could hardly wait to meet
his friends and try his new trick.
He could count to ten!

Drip.

Drip.

Drip.

"Oh, no!" cried Hopsalot.
"We can't play outside in the rain!"

Hopsalot tapped his foot.
"I know!" he said. "I'll have a
party and count to ten right here."

Eleanor came first.
She brought a book.
"Great!" said Hopsalot.
"I count ONE book."

Pierre came next.
"I love puddles!" he said.
"Me, too!" said Hopsalot.
"I count TWO puddles."

Casey followed — on his hands!
"Silly cat!" Hopsalot laughed.
"I count THREE red balls.
I count FOUR green balls."

Frankie came next and brought his lunch.

"FIVE bones!" said Hopsalot.

CJ and Edison followed Frankie.
"SIX emeralds!" Hopsalot said.
"SEVEN pencils!"

Kisha came last.
"EIGHT paintbrushes!"
"NINE buckets of paint!"

Everyone looked outside.
"Rain, rain, go away!"
Kisha sang.
"Come again some other day!"
That gave Hopsalot an idea.
"Let's paint a sunny day!"
he shouted.

And that's just what they did.

Everyone was happy, but Kisha said, "Something is missing."

"Look!" Edison shouted.
The rain had stopped.
A rainbow was shining in the sky.

"Now I know what's missing!" said Kisha. "A beautiful rainbow."

"Look! Now it's a sunny day inside *and* outside," Kisha said.
"Playing together is fun," said Hopsalot. Then he ran outside and jumped in a big puddle.

"One, two, three, four, five,
six, seven, eight, nine, ten drops!"
Hops shouted.
"Great job, Hopsalot!" cried the gang.
"You can count to ten!"
Counting is fun in the rain or sun!